Discrd

W9-CPV-343

Pasquala of Santa Ynez Mission

Pasquala of

Santa Ynez Mission

Florence Wightman Rowland

illustrated by Charles Geer

New York | *Henry Z. Walck, Inc.* | *1961*

To Ann Leflang
and her daughter, Cathy Sue

Contents

1 Will There Be Trouble? *1*

2 The Unfriendly Indian *10*

3 The Biggest Fish *20*

4 Harvest Fiesta *29*

5 The Feathered Warning *37*

6 The Wedding Shawl *44*

7 The Piñons Are Ripe *52*

8 The Christmas Play *65*

9 The Arrow Race *73*

10 The Captive *83*

11 The Warpath *90*

12 The Long Journey *99*

13 The Message for Father Uria *106*

Pasquala of Santa Ynez Mission

1 | *Will There Be Trouble?*

Tucking the food bowl under one arm, Pasquala followed the winding path that led to the Mission Santa Ynez. Overhead, the aged oak and pepper trees grew close together. They cast dark shadows across the narrow trail shutting out the bright California sun.

As Pasquala hurried along, she tried to shake off a feeling of gloom; but she could not. She had much to worry her this morning.

Only yesterday, her uncle, chief of the Tulare Indian tribe, had warned Pasquala's father again. For the fifth time his messenger had brought the same threat: *"Return to the tribal village, or there will be trouble!"*

Pasquala's dark eyes filled with despair. Would there be trouble? Early each spring, her uncle sent one of his young braves to speak these evil words. Angry because his brother's family had become Christians, he wanted them to leave the peaceful life of mission Indians. He wanted them to accept again the pagan beliefs of their own people.

But there had been no real peace for Pasquala or her parents during the five years they had been at Santa Ynez. They had never felt really safe.

Following the sharp bend in the footpath, Pasquala sighed. They did not want to return to the tribe. So far they had paid no attention to the threats. And so far no harm had come to their family. But Pasquala knew that something might happen at any time.

Through a sudden gap between the huge trees, Pasquala caught sight of the high Santa Ynez Mountains to the north. She knew that the village of the Tulare Indians lay far away behind the tall peaks. She did not want to live there ever again. She loved the mission. She wondered if she and her parents would be forced to leave the peaceful ways of the mission and the teachings of their kind Padre, Father Uria. With her whole heart, she wanted to stay forever.

A sudden noise of snapping twigs broke into Pasquala's thoughts. She smiled when she saw her friend, Jorge. Already fourteen years old, he had almost reached his full height. Although she was tall for ten

years, Pasquala scarcely came up to his broad shoulders.

Leaping over a fallen log, Jorge fell in step with her. He wore only a loincloth and carried two large food bowls. A red headband kept his black hair out of his dark eyes.

Shivering in the chilly spring air, Pasquala asked, "Aren't you cold?"

"No."

"But the air feels cool to me," she insisted.

"That's because you're a girl," he teased. Then he went on. "I'll be glad when summer comes."

"I'll be glad too," Pasquala said. "I like to hunt berries."

"Spear fishing's the most fun."

Wistfully, Pasquala said, "I've never gone."

"It is not for girls," Jorge answered, his voice full of scorn. "Spears are too heavy for you to throw. Your hands were made to hold a needle."

But stubbornly Pasquala thought: "Someday I'll catch a fish with a spear, and then won't Jorge be surprised?"

As Pasquala walked up the narrow path, her full blue skirt brushed her beaded moccasins. Her two long, black braids swung back and forth behind her at each graceful step.

Pasquala glanced at the large bowls Jorge carried. It took much food to feed his big family. He had four younger brothers and sisters still at home.

Margarita, his oldest sister, no longer stayed in the hut of her parents. She lived in one of the large buildings with the other unmarried girls. And his oldest brother, Luis, stayed in the special rooms for the single young men. In four more years, when he became eighteen, Jorge would live there, too, until he married.

Before long, they saw the red-tiled roofs of the white mission buildings gleaming in the bright sunlight. Pasquala and Jorge went through the main gate and along the south corridor. Soon they came to the big kitchen. Near the open door were many boys and girls. Each carried one or two pottery bowls, depending on the size of the family. Pasquala heard their gay voices as they chatted, waiting their turns.

Soon their bowls had been filled with hot chili beans in beef sauce. Pasquala sniffed the spicy odor and urged, "Let's hurry, Jorge. I'm so hungry."

Pasquala and Jorge walked back together until the turnoff where Jorge left Pasquala to follow the path to his own home. As she walked on alone, she thought of how different the ways of the mission were from those of her tribe.

Pasquala loved Santa Ynez because her father no longer went on long hunting trips to kill bear or puma. He no longer sharpened spears and arrows, or made heavy war clubs.

Ever since leaving their tribal village, Pasquala's father had been kind and gentle. Their family had gladly accepted the words of peace and love taught by Father Uria.

This great change in her father brought much happiness to Pasquala's mother. She smiled as she worked, grateful that her husband would not go on the warpath ever again.

Pasquala often remembered how they had come to live at this mission. When she was five years old, she had become quite ill. Old Nau-kloo, the medicine man of the Tulares, sang many chants to drive out the evil spirits. But Pasquala's fever had grown worse with each passing hour.

Watching her getting weaker and weaker, her father finally recalled something important. A member of their tribe had once told him that mission padres could make sick people well. This special magic of the mission Fathers could even cool fevers.

When Pasquala's father had first heard this, he had dismissed it as nonsense, having more faith in their medicine man. But, frantic with worry, he was willing to try anything that might save his child's life.

So he carried Pasquala over the high mountain trails to Santa Ynez, the nearest mission. Having once defied old Nau-kloo, he dared not turn back. The wrath of the medicine man was something to be feared.

And Pasquala was cured. When Father Uria invited them to stay there, her parents quickly accepted his offer. They willingly gave up their tribal beliefs to live close to the walls of the mission among other Indian families.

When Father Uria baptized her, he changed her Indian name, Noktu, to Pasquala. She liked her Christian name, for it meant "one who helps other people."

Now, as Pasquala hurried toward the hut of her parents, she could not push aside the disturbing thoughts that filled her mind. She knew that her uncle, as chief of the tribe, expected to be obeyed. He did not want them to follow the ways of the white man. He scoffed at his brother's being a grower of grapes instead of a bold warrior.

In the mission schoolroom, the good Padre often told his pupils, "Even in this year of 1819, many men have not yet learned to live together in peace." When she heard this, Pasquala wished the fierce Tulares could be taught to understand the gentle teachings of Father Uria, to "love thy neighbor."

Almost at the end of the winding path, Pasquala frowned again, remembering how one of her uncle's braves had crept up behind her father the afternoon before, as he worked in the vineyard. The young Indian came to speak the usual command: *"Return to the tribal village, or there will be trouble!"*

During the night, voices from the other room had awakened Pasquala. Lying on her bed mat near the open door, she had listened to her mother's anxious words. "But *this* time your brother may harm you. *This* time he may send a feathered warning!"

A feathered warning!

Pasquala trembled with fright. She knew what that meant. The most feared custom was a feathered warning. When it was tossed at the door of anyone who did not obey the chief, death came soon after from poisoned arrows.

How brave, how sensible Pasquala's father had been. She would never forget his calm reply. He had not sounded afraid or worried. "My brother speaks empty words," he told his wife. "He has sent this same message to me five times. Is this not so? Still no harm has come to us. He only wants to frighten us." After a pause, he went on, "I say there is nothing to fear. Would he kill his own brother? I suspect old Nau-kloo is behind these threats. Old Nau-kloo, the evil one."

Remembering this conversation now, Pasquala's heart beat faster and faster. It thumped against her ribs making it hard for her to breathe.

As she stepped through the open door of her home, Pasquala asked herself again: "*Was* there nothing to fear?"

She ate the hot food she had brought from the mission kitchen and tried to forget her gloomy thoughts. But after, on the way to the schoolroom, she still felt upset and uneasy because of the dreadful thing that could happen to them now.

2 | *The Unfriendly Indian*

TRYING to shake off her feeling of gloom, Pasquala hurried toward the mission buildings. But the dark shadows across the winding path made her quite uneasy. Every tree could hide an unfriendly Indian.

At the sound of snapping twigs, Pasquala stood still, her heart beating wildly. She listened. The noise had stopped. Perhaps it had been a chipmunk scampering among the dry leaves in search of acorns.

Pasquala kept on, glancing back once in a while, relieved when she saw no one on the trail. She would have felt safer with Jorge there, or his friends Pablo and Fernando.

Pasquala went faster and faster. Not until she dashed through the main gate did she breathe easily. Gratefully, she fell in step with the noisy boys and girls hurrying along the north corridor.

Pasquala entered the large, sunny room and sank down on the nearest bench, next to her friend, Rosa.

Staring at her, the chubby girl asked, "Something wrong? You look scared to death."

Pasquala did not want anyone outside her family to know about the latest threat, or the possibility that a feathered warning might be thrown on their doorstep. She forced herself to smile. "I walked fast," she answered. "I was late. I'm out of breath." This much was true, and her explanation satisfied Rosa. She smiled back at Pasquala.

Father Uria entered the schoolroom and the children stood up, waiting for his greeting.

"Good morning, boys and girls."

"Good morning, Father Uria," they chorused.

When they had sat down again, their Padre told them in a kind voice, "I am leaving our mission on a foot journey. I hope to bring back many Indians to live with us at Santa Ynez."

As he spoke, Pasquala noticed that he wore a leather jacket made of deerskin. He always put this over his brown robes when he went away. In spite of its thickness, she knew it would not protect him from poisoned arrows.

Every time their Padre left the mission to convert Indians to Christianity, he carried a cross in one hand and a Bible in the other. Under his arm, in a small cloth bag, he had a loaf of dark bread, an extra pair of sandals and many strings of bright beads to win over unfriendly Indians.

"There will be no lessons until I return," Father Uria said. The children nudged each other and grinned.

But Pasquala was disappointed. She looked forward each morning to the stories their Padre told them before he assigned the work for the day. She especially enjoyed hearing about Father Esteban Tapis and how he had founded the mission fifteen years before, in 1804. She also enjoyed the religious studies and the singing classes, and the new Spanish words they learned to pronounce each day.

But most of all, Pasquala never tired of hearing about their patron saint, Santa Ynez. Father Uria told this story so well, so vividly, that Pasquala could almost see the little child who became Saint Agnes. Father Tapis had named the mission afer her.

Father Uria's voice interrupted Pasquala's thoughts. He said, "Jorge will take the younger boys to chase the birds away from the wheat plants. If the birds eat the tender stalks, the wheat will die. Should that happen, there will be little food for us this winter."

Jorge stood up. Motioning to the boys in the first three rows, he said, "Come!"

After they left, Father Uria spoke to Fernando. "Take the older boys with you. Go to the leather shops and the blacksmith and the soap and metal workers. The men there will find chores for you all."

Pasquala felt Father Uria's eyes on her. She hoped he would choose her. But he looked away. Then he turned back to speak to Rosa.

"Take the girls to the weaving and sewing rooms, Rosa," he directed. "And to Lucia in the kitchen. There is much to be done."

The girls trooped out of the schoolroom. Pasquala walked beside Rosa. At each place, a few girls stayed behind to work at the looms, or with needle and thread. When only six were left in the group, Rosa went with them to the last building behind all of the others. This was where the food was prepared.

Pasquala looked up to see a plump, friendly woman standing in the doorway. Lucia, head of the kitchen, waited. Briskly, she said, "There is a pestle and mortar for four of you. And here is a bowl of seed to pound smooth."

All except Rosa and Pasquala picked up the pounding

bowls. Lucia spoke to them. "You two will clean this seed for me. It needs careful sorting and washing." She handed them each a large basket filled to the brim.

Pasquala and Rosa began to pick out the small pebbles and bits of twigs. The tedious work took a long time. When the seed was finally ready to wash, Pasquala and Rosa picked up jugs made of pottery. They walked up the path to the big reservoir not far from the north mission walls.

They dipped out some water and started back, carrying the heavy pitchers on their shoulders. Pasquala knew that mountain streams kept the reservoir full. She could see the deep ditches that led out from it. Through these the water went to the far-off grape arbors and to the olive trees. It even went as far as the orange and lemon orchards, and to the grain fields and vegetable gardens. In the dry months, when the rains did not fall, this reservoir was very important to the mission. It provided drinking water for those who lived there. It also kept growing things alive at the end of the long, hot southern California summers, when the Santa Ynez River was usually too low to be used for the irrigation of crops.

As Pasquala reached the doorway, Lucia called to her from inside the big kitchen. "I forgot to tell you, Pasquala, but Jorge's mother needs someone to watch the baby while she works. It is wash day. She asked for you especially. Rosa can finish your seed."

It did not take Pasquala long to reach the river. As she followed along the banks of the tumbling stream, she heard the sound of laughter and talking not far away.

She found Jorge's mother kneeling at her work. "Lucia sent me to take care of the baby," she said.

"It is good you came," the woman said. "You know how to hush him." She nodded toward a small basket cradle near an old oak tree.

Pasquala watched the woman rub a wet shirt against a flat stone and then splash the garment up and down in the swift river. After that, she twisted it a time or two to squeeze out the water. Shaking out the wrinkles, she spread it over a nearby bush to dry in the sun.

Glad to tend the baby, Pasquala turned away eagerly. He was crying softly as she leaned down to pick him up. "There, there," she soothed, laying him against her shoulder. When she touched one of his tiny hands, it felt softer than the velvet altar cloths that she helped to brush each week.

Walking up and down to quiet him, Pasquala sang a lullaby known as the "Sleepy Sparrow" by her people.

Her mother had sung it to her long before while they still lived with their tribe.

After a while, the baby fell asleep. Carefully, Pasquala laid him down in his cradle and covered him with the soft blanket. She sat down next to him in case he cried again, but Jorge's little brother did not awaken until the sun shone directly overhead. The air now filled with the clear sound of the mission bells, calling everyone to midday prayers.

After the baby's mother had thanked her and started up the trail with him, Pasquala hurried home to get her shawl to cover her head in church.

A sudden movement in the dark path startled Pasquala. From among the black shadows just ahead of her, a slender Indian leaped out from behind an oak tree.

"Noktu!" He spat out the word angrily, his eyes full of hatred.

Pasquala gasped in terror. She could not move. The Indian had called her by her tribal name! She recognized him almost at once, although she had not seen him for five years. He had been just a half-grown youth then in their tribal village. Now, he was a tall young warrior.

When Pasquala did not say anything, he went on in the language of the Tulares. "Will you answer to your Christian name, *Pasquala?*"

Trembling, Pasquala decided to ignore him as her father would have done. Bravely, she started to pass him on the narrow trail. But he moved, too, so that he always blocked her way. She could not get by him.

Finally, the young man spoke again. "Your father is foolish. He does not believe his brother. Why have you not left the mission? I spoke the warning. Does your father think our chief is weak and should not be obeyed?"

In despair, Pasquala stood looking at him. He was painted for the warpath. His youthful face had streaks of yellow and red stripes across it from ear to ear and from forehead to chin. He looked fierce and dangerous.

Pasquala's mouth was so dry from fright she could not have answered him even if she had wanted to. Besides, it had been so long since she had spoken their language that she was not sure of the words.

Realizing Pasquala was not going to argue with him, the tall brave went as suddenly as he had leaped out at her. He strode off through the thick growth of pepper trees to the north and disappeared from sight. Pasquala knew he was headed for the village of the Tulares behind the high Santa Ynez Mountains.

Still trembling, Pasquala reached home. Later, her heart continued to beat wildly as she sat beside her mother on the women's side of the church.

So far Pasquala had been able to hide her troubled thoughts from her parents. She stared at the bright sunlight spilling over the seven-foot-high window sills, built higher than a tall man's head to keep poisoned arrows from harming those inside. Several raids had already been made against other California missions. So far Santa Ynez had escaped.

Still worried, Pasquala stared straight ahead into the gentle face of the child saint, Santa Ynez. The small statue stood in the narrow alcove above the altar. Whenever she looked at Saint Agnes, Pasquala felt peaceful.

But today, no peace filled her heart. She could still see too clearly the fierce face of the young warrior and hear his angry words. She wondered if she should tell her parents. She wondered what her uncle would do now. After hearing that his brother's family had not left Santa Ynez, would he send a feathered warning?

3 | *The Biggest Fish*

PASQUALA could not forget the fierce young brave who had jumped out at her. But the warm spring days had changed to those full of summer's dry heat, and still he had not come back.

This afternoon, Pasquala hurried toward the red-tiled roofs of the mission buildings. She did not want to be late for the singing class she enjoyed so much. She often wished that girls could be in the church choir; but only boys were chosen.

Once, when she asked her mother why this was so, her mother had answered, "It is the way of the mission. You must not question the wisdom of our Padre. He only follows the custom handed down through the years. It is something we must accept, even though we do not understand why."

As Pasquala crossed the patio, she saw two boys half hidden by a large rosebush near Father Uria's private garden. They were Jorge and Fernando. They carried fishing spears. The pleased looks on their faces told her of the fun they looked forward to having.

Pasquala ran over to them. "Oh, Jorge," she begged, "take me too?"

Fernando scowled. "I knew she'd see us," he snapped, glaring at her. "I knew she'd want to go with us."

A mischievous smile on his face, Jorge teased, "You'd only be a nuisance, Pasquala. It takes the strong arm of a *man* to throw a spear. Your hands were made to hold a needle."

Before Pasquala could protest, Fernando snorted, "Who ever heard of a girl spearing a fish?"

Pasquala did not answer. She pouted, knowing they would not let her go along no matter what she said. Since the boys would not take her with them, she was determined to go by herself. She would prove to them that girls could handle a spear and catch fish too.

Forgetting all about the singing class, Pasquala turned away and dashed back across the patio again without further argument.

Jorge called after her, "Who'll sing the high notes if you are not there?"

Pasquala did not answer him. She did not even turn around. Excitedly, she hurried up the trail. This time she scarcely noticed the dark shadows across the narrow, winding path.

Pasquala went behind the small hut where her father kept his spears. He had three. Each had a sharp, pointed end. At the other a long strip of leather dangled from the shaft. She knew her father tied this thong to his wrist while fishing. It kept the spear from being lost in the swift river.

Pasquala chose the shortest spear, knowing the others

would be too heavy to throw. Even so, it tired her out long before she reached the place where the two boys stood at the edge of the steep bank.

Cautiously, Pasquala crept through the thick bushes, not wanting Jorge or Fernando to see her just yet. She decided to catch a fish first. Then, when she showed it to them, they would have to admit that girls could fish with spears too. If she caught nothing, there was no need for them to ever know that she had tried.

Pasquala chose a small cove beyond the bend in the river. She stood as close to the edge as she dared and looked down into the Santa Ynez. The water was still quite deep. Only at the end of the summer did it lose its swiftness and become shallow.

It was more difficult than Pasquala had thought to tie the leather strip to her right wrist. But, somehow, she finally knotted the stiff piece of leather in place. Then she held the spear ready to throw. Suddenly she saw something silvery flash through the water. One after another the fish swam past her. Seeing an unusually large one, she thrust the heavy spear forward.

ZING!

Like something alive, the spear sprang downward. But, at that instant, Pasquala froze. Her eye had caught a sudden movement in the distance. Three shadowy figures crept down the narrow mountain trail. She stared at them, shading her eyes against the sun's bright glare, trying to see who they were. She felt a growing uneasiness. Was it just her imagination, or did the tallest Indian look like her uncle?

Dismayed, Pasquala wished the sunlight would not dance so brightly upon the trail. She could not be sure if the man was her father's brother, because the shimmering spots of sun almost blinded her.

Pasquala watched them until they finally disappeared behind the thick bushes at the edge of the flat valley. How she wished she had recognized them as Indians from Santa Ynez, returning from the high mountain valley where the mission sheep grazed.

Trying to get a last look at them as they turned toward the mission buildings, Pasquala forgot where she was and stepped forward. She felt her foot begin to slip over the edge of the steep bank. She pulled back, but it was too late. Losing her balance, she slid toward the river. She grabbed a large stone, and it stopped her downward plunge. But only for a moment. It finally loosened with her weight and started rolling. Pasquala let go and heard it splash into the water.

She gasped as she fell into the river. She bobbed up and yelled for help, but no sound came. Her mouth

was full of water. As the strong current pulled her along, the weight of her wet clothes kept dragging her under.

Splashing desperately with her hands, Pasquala struggled to the surface once more. She knew how to swim, but the river carried her along too fast for her to get close enough to the muddy bank to climb up.

Then she saw Jorge running along the edge of the slope just above her. Fernando was right behind him.

Flinging himself headfirst, Jorge dived in close to her. He grabbed her arm and began pulling her toward

the place where Fernando stood waiting to help them. He leaned out over the water, holding a long spear in his hands.

He yelled, "Get it, Jorge."

Jorge leaped up and grabbed hold of the end of the shaft with one hand. With the other, he held on to Pasquala. "Be quick," he urged, guiding the spear closer to her outstretched fingers.

Pasquala felt sick from the water she had swallowed, but she grabbed the spear.

"Climb up!" Fernando yelled.

With Jorge pushing from behind and Fernando pulling from the high bank, Pasquala made her way step by step slippery step up the muddy slope. The heavy spear still fastened to her wrist kept dragging her backwards.

After she was safe, Fernando pulled Jorge up too.

For a while Pasquala lay on the ground too tired to move. Her stomach was swollen, and it felt tight as a drum. When she pressed her hands against it, groaning, Fernando reached for her. He rolled her over and over and back again.

At first, she did not understand his rough treatment; but the water spilled from her mouth, and afterwards she felt much better.

Jorge sounded cross when he said, "Maybe now

you'll believe me when I say spear fishing is not for girls. They haven't enough sense not to fall into the river."

Pasquala did not answer him. She could not tell him about the Indians she had seen on the trail, and how she thought the tallest one had looked like her uncle. Jorge would think she was making excuses. Besides, she did not want him to know about the latest threat, or the feathered warning, either. It was enough that her own family had to worry about this without bothering others with tribal difficulties.

Blinking water from her eyes, Pasquala saw Fernando grin. He leaned over to unfasten the strip of leather still tied to her wrist. He stood up and walked to where the spear lay.

He said, "You caught a fish, Pasquala." He held it up for her to see. It was as long as his hand. "It's quite big," he admitted, "but it isn't half as big as the one Jorge caught."

Disappointed, Pasquala looked around. "I don't see any fish," she said crossly. "Where's Jorge's?"

The boys laughed at her question.

Jorge stopped long enough to explain. "Fernando's right, Pasquala. I did catch a bigger fish. I caught you, didn't I?"

In spite of herself, Pasquala laughed too.

Later, Pasquala proudly carried her fish home. But she could not forget the tall Indian she had seen on the mountain trail, or her fear that it had been her uncle.

ONE autumn morning, just before dawn, Pasquala lay on her bed mat listening to the sweet music of the mission bells, chiming the call to prayers. When they stopped ringing, she threw off her blanket, not wanting to be late.

A short while later, Pasquala followed her parents as they went up the path toward the mission gate. On both sides of the narrow trail she saw the deep reds and soft yellows of the changing leaves. These beautiful colors made October the prettiest month of all.

Pasquala liked autumn. It was the time of the Harvest Fiesta. She always looked forward to the special celebrations when everyone gave thanks for the abundant crops.

But Pasquala had a good reason to dread this season, too. During the fall the piñon nuts ripened. It was then that Father Uria sent most of the women and children up the long trail to the pine forest, high up in the Santa Ynez Mountains. The plump, sweet nuts made good food for those who lived at the mission, and everyone enjoyed their delicious flavor.

Each year, Pasquala and her mother, along with the other women and girls and the smaller boys, climbed up the steep trail to fill large bags with the brown nuts. The children especially liked this holiday away from chores—all but Pasquala. The pine forest was too close to the village of the Tulare Indians to suit her. If one of her tribe were to see them, it was possible that she and her mother would be forced to go back to the Indian village. Her father would not be able to help them; he would be far away in the mission vineyard tending to the grapes.

Pushing aside these thoughts, Pasquala remembered gratefully that this was an especially good year for the olives, the various fruits and the many vegetables. She knew there would be no hungry Indians during the winter at Santa Ynez. Much food had already been stored away in stout bins behind thick adobe brick walls and under red-tiled roofs. These would protect the harvest from the heavy rains and cold winds that usually came in January and February.

At the door of the church, Pasquala met Jorge. Evidently he had waited for her. He smiled, a look of importance on his face.

Eagerly, he explained, "I am to help the men in the fields today. Father Uria said I am a man almost. My father gave me his next-to-largest sickle."

"I am glad," Pasquala said, proud of him.

During the morning, Pasquala and the other girls kept busy carrying water to quench the thirst of the men working in the fields. They made many trips to the reservoir to fill the water jugs. As fast as Pasquala and the other girls brought the heavy pitchers to the harvesters, the thirsty men and boys emptied them. By noon, she was very tired.

She ate two corn pancakes and drank a cup full of thick, sweet chocolate, looking forward to siesta time, the hour after eating when everyone at the mission rested from his chores.

It seemed but a moment after Pasquala lay down on her bed mat and closed her eyes that someone shook her gently by the shoulder. Her mother urged, "Come, Pasquala. It is time to go back to the fields. But by the

time the Angelus calls us from our labors, the grain will be harvested. Then we can enjoy the gay fiesta."

During the long afternoon, Pasquala stopped several times to watch Jorge as his arm swung back and forth. She was glad that he kept up with the men. His naked back shone with sweat. He rested only long enough to drink some of the cool water from her jug.

At last, the workers began to arrange the last four sheaves from the field. Pasquala watched as Jorge and Fernando held these in place while their fathers tied them together with leather thongs. It was the custom that the last four bundles of wheat were formed into a cross and carried to the church to start the fiesta.

Jorge and Fernando lifted the cross of wheat between them. The other reapers laid aside their sharp sickles and followed the boys over the bare ground through the main gate and up to the carved wooden door of the church.

Pasquala heard the mission bells chiming. They seemed to say, "It is the harvest. Be merry! Be merry! Be thankful! Be thankful!"

Rosa and Pasquala joined the long line of Indians as they followed Jorge and Fernando. Father Uria stood in the doorway. Teodoro and Pablo and many more Indian boys grouped together nearby, singing a chant of thanksgiving.

Pasquala knew it well. She hummed softly as the workers moved slowly down the center aisle. Then she and Rosa found seats toward the back of the crowded church. The Harvest Fiesta had begun.

After the evening meal, it was time for the games. Standing on the sidelines, Pasquala watched the boys at the stone toss. When it was Fernando's turn, he stepped up to the line and aimed carefully.

Pasquala wondered how anyone could throw a heavy stone that far, although she secretly wished that girls could take part too. But they were expected to watch the fun.

Three times Fernando threw a stone toward the large circle; but each time it rolled outside the lines scraped into the bare ground. Boy after boy stepped forward, only to throw too short or too far.

Finally, it was Jorge's turn. Pasquala saw how eager he was, and she hoped he would win. Breathlessly, she watched as he threw first one stone, then another. Both went too far. But the third stone wobbled over and over and came to a stop near the center of the circle.

Jorge had won!

Smiling happily, Jorge walked toward her a moment later. Proudly, he held out his prize, three bright pebbles. One pink, one green and the other white.

How they sparkled! Pasquala reached out to touch them. She ran a finger over their smooth sides. Looking at them in his open palm brought back memories for her. She remembered as if it had been yesterday the long trip her tribe made each year to the Sunset Ocean. There they gathered sea shells and pebbles such as these that Jorge had won. The Tulares used them as money when trading with other tribes.

Besides this, they had another important use for them. Her uncle always marked the trail to the ocean with white pebbles. Since it was easy to lose the way through the mountains, he set three large pebbles at the base of a tree at each fork in the long, twisting trail. By following them, the leaders never missed reaching the coast. They returned to their tribal village the same way, guided by the markers.

Pasquala had never found pebbles on the beach as pretty as these.

After the games ended, Pasquala and Teresa helped

to serve the sweets made in the kitchen for the Harvest Fiesta. Later on, nibbling a piece of honey cake filled with chopped walnut meats, Pasquala looked around at the smiling faces. Contentment shone in everyone's eyes. Life at the mission was peaceful and good.

5 | *The Feathered Warning*

THE morning after the Harvest Fiesta, Pasquala stopped to watch Luis and several other young men thresh the grain. With great skill, they raced their swift horses around and around over piles of freshly cut grain thrown on the hard ground.

Standing beside her, Jorge boasted, "My brother rides better than anyone."

"He certainly does," Pasquala agreed loyally.

It was almost frightening to hear Luis crack the long whip to make the horses gallop even faster. After they ran one way for a while, the men turned them around to run in the opposite direction.

Pasquala clung to the rough boards that closed in the threshing area. "Won't the horses break down the fence?" she asked.

"No, it's strong," Jorge assured her. "Besides, Luis will keep the horses inside where they belong. My brother won't let them hurt anyone."

On the other side of Pasquala, Carmen, Fernando's youngest sister, squatted in the dirt. She watched the racing animals, her eyes bright with excitement.

In about an hour, the grain had been forced out of the husks. Now that their work was done, the men guided their horses out of the field. The women and children gathered up the grain and carried it to the large storage bins in a nearby building.

A few days later, Pasquala sat in the schoolroom with the other children. Father Uria said, "Pedro, our master candlemaker, asked me to send three girls to help him. I promised to choose those who are quick and careful. He has ceremonial candles to dip."

"Ceremonial candles are important," Pasquala thought. "We need so many of them. In the church two tall candles burn constantly through every hour of the day and night. They light up the sweet face of Saint Agnes in her niche above the altar."

All the girls hoped to be chosen. Pasquala knew that the last time she helped Pedro he had said he was pleased with her work. She hoped the old candlemaker had told their Padre that she was quick to learn.

Father Uria spoke first to Sara. She stood up quickly, her face showing her delight.

Then the Padre glanced past Pasquala and said, "Laura!"

Pasquala tried not to show her disappointment. Both Sara and Laura were new pupils. Neither had ever helped Pedro before, and they had been chosen.

"Pasquala!"

The sound of her own name made her jump up so fast that all the children laughed. But she did not mind.

"Y-yes, Father," she said excitedly.

"The last time you helped Pedro I heard many kind words about you, Pasquala. He said you have steady hands. But what is even more important than that, he said you have patience too. So, you will teach both Laura and Sara. Pedro is too busy to do that. I want these new girls to be as fine candle dippers as you are."

Pleased at this praise, Pasquala said modestly, "I'll do my best."

"I am sure of that," their Padre answered solemnly. "Run along, now. Pedro needs you."

The three girls left the schoolroom and hurried up the south corridor to the candle shop. Old Pedro waited for them. He smiled. "It is good that you have come,

Pasquala. We will make straight, smooth candles with you to do the dipping."

Laura and Sara peeped into the large kettle that hung over the big fire just outside the room where the candles would be made. Pedro told them how the water and tallow had been mixed together. The liquid boiled merrily.

"I have already skimmed it two times," he told them. "While it cooks you should finish twisting the wicks on the candle rods. The dipping cannot begin until the job is done."

The girls chatted while they worked. Pasquala showed Laura and Sara how to get started on the shorter candles, as soon as the tallow was ready. Each wick had to be dipped into the hot liquid, then hung on the rod by the loop on one end. After each had dried thoroughly, it was again lowered into the fat. This was repeated over and over until the candle became big enough.

When she saw that the girls were learning, Pasquala turned to the long ceremonial candles. She tried to keep her hand steady as she lowered the longer wick into the melted tallow and carefully hung it up to dry.

Once in a while Pedro came and stood beside her, watching what she did. Finally, he said, "You do fine.

You make them straight and true. Have you noticed the day, Pasquala?"

"Yes," she answered. "It is cool enough and damp enough. The candles will not dry out too fast and become brittle."

Pedro nodded his head up and down, smiling. "It could not be better for the ceremonial candles. We shall both be proud of the candles we make this day."

The girls worked steadily. Hour after hour passed swiftly. At noon they went to the kitchen and asked Lucia for a bowl of chili beans and some corn pancakes. Then they went back to their dipping.

When the shorter candles were finished, Laura and Sara left for home, but Pasquala stayed to finish up the few she had already started.

These took longer than she had thought; but when they were finally hung up to dry, she said good-by to Pedro and hurried toward the mission gate. The coming night made the narrow path black with shadows, and she felt uneasy. She began to run and did not stop until she reached her own door.

No candlelight poured through the open windows; her mother had not yet come home from the mission sewing room. For some reason her father must have been delayed at the vineyards.

As Pasquala stepped into the dark room, her moccasin kicked something to one side. Her heart pounded against her ribs. She told herself that what she kicked could be a stick of wood her father dropped when he fixed the broken stool that morning. It could be a bunch of the reed her mother often gathered for basket weaving.

Pasquala stooped down. In the dim light, her hand searched along the dirt floor. Directly in front of her, her groping fingers touched the bundle of feathers and bleached bones.

The warning had come!

6 | *The Wedding Shawl*

THE day after Pasquala found the feathered warning, she waited at the church to speak to Jorge. She put her shawl over her head, covering up her long braids.

Standing there, she saw how the bright sunlight lit up the red-tiled roofs and the thick, white adobe walls of the mission buildings. It was a peaceful scene, but Pasquala's heart was far from peaceful.

Not for one moment could she forget the bundle of feathers and bleached bones. She had hidden it under her blankets so that her parents would not see it.

Pasquala wondered if she should tell them it had come. But perhaps, if she did, her father would decide to go back to the tribal village. That must not happen! Or if she should tell Father Uria. She had decided against that. She would first show Jorge the feathered warning and ask his advice.

Pasquala did not see Jorge among the boys coming toward the church, but she met his oldest sister, Margarita. The slender young girl smiled at her, and Pasquala saw that her eyes shone like the stars in a clear heaven.

Margarita said, "Listen, Pasquala. There will be something spoken this morning that will be a surprise."

"Tell me now," Pasquala begged. "I can't wait."

Margarita laughed merrily and shook her head. "No, you will hear what it is soon enough."

They went into the church together and found a place to sit. Pasquala looked across the aisle and saw Juan, Rafael and Miguel. They had just returned from Santa Barbara. They had driven oxcarts piled high with cured hides and had exchanged the hides for the many things needed at Santa Ynez.

Pasquala was glad they had returned safely. The long mountain trail was full of dangers. Often hostile Indians stopped the carts, killing the drivers and stealing what they could.

When the time came for Father Uria to make the announcements, he named those about to be married.

Three Sundays in a row the banns would be spoken by
their Padre. After that, the chapel would be decorated
with flowers, many candles lit, and the ceremony would
take place.

"The first banns of Margarita and Juan."

Pasquala gasped in surprise. Glancing at the young
girl beside her, Pasquala saw at once it was true. Margarita's cheeks were pink as she glanced across the aisle
at Juan.

Pasquala was delighted. Margarita and Juan! So that

was the secret. No wonder Margarita looked so happy. And Juan too.

Soon their names would be written down in the book of records. And some day, Pasquala's name and the name of her husband would be there too.

Pasquala paid little attention to what happened after that. She was far too excited. As the last notes of the choir ended, she hurried outside to be one in the crowd that congratulated Margarita and Juan.

Suddenly Pasquala remembered that she wanted to speak to Jorge. As soon as she could, she left the group and started up the trail to look for Jorge.

That day and the next Pasquala did not see him. He was not in the schoolroom; probably Father Uria had sent him on some task.

It was not until late Tuesday afternoon that Pasquala saw Jorge. He sat on a fallen log, whittling. She hurried home to get the warning, and a few moments later she came back to where Jorge was.

"Are we alone?" she asked, looking around cautiously.

"Alone?" he answered, a grin on his face. "Must we talk where only the silent forest may listen?"

"I want to show you something," Pasquala began, pulling the feathered warning out from under her apron where she had hidden it. "Look! My uncle sent this." She handed him the ugly thing and told him how she found the bundle of feathers and bones on their doorstep and about the five warnings that had come.

Jorge kept turning it over, frowning. "So this is a feathered warning," he said. "I have never seen one before. We of the Chumash tribe do not make them."

"Will there be trouble, Jorge?"

The boy shrugged his broad shoulders. "Who can know that?" he said. "But I believe as your father believes. Your uncle is just trying to frighten you. He wants you to return to the tribe."

Pasquala felt a little better. "Then, I am not to worry?"

Jorge looked quite solemn. "Only your uncle knows what is in his mind," he replied quietly. "But the walls of our mission are high. And strong. They will protect you. Have you forgotten the soldiers that are here to keep hostile Indians from harming us?"

"That is true," Pasquala agreed. "The soldiers are here to guard us."

Jorge stood up and looked around. "We'll bury this ugly thing here. The forest will keep our secret. If I were you, Pasquala, I would not tell your parents about this. It would only worry them."

The next weeks flew by for Pasquala and Margarita. They were kept busy fixing up the adobe brick hut that Juan had built for Margarita and himself. It stood on the edge of the cluster of homes, not far from where Pasquala lived. She was glad of that.

The two girls hung up the curtains at the windows and spread the pretty blankets on the sleeping mats. Margarita brought several colorful jugs and reed baskets. She put these around the two rooms.

On the day the third banns were announced, Pasquala and Margarita hurried to the home that would be Juan's and Margarita's after they were married. A large box sat in the middle of the dirt floor near the door.

Margarita smiled at Pasquala. "I have something to show you. You'll be the first to see my wedding shawl. I wove it myself." Proudly, she opened the lid, her eyes bright with happiness.

Inside lay a fine shawl. Pasquala leaned over to touch it. "It's beautiful, Margarita. Just beautiful. I hope some-day to learn how to weave smoothly like that."

"You will," Margarita answered, draping the shawl over Pasquala's arm. "Now we'll get your shawl."

"Mine?"

"Yes, yours!" Margarita leaned over the box again. She lifted out a second shawl, smaller than hers, but

exactly like it in pattern and design. It was made from the same fine wool yarn. "This is for you. As my flower girl you must have a pretty shawl too."

Pasquala gasped in delight. "Oh, thank you! Thank you, Margarita." She hugged her friend. "I can hardly believe it."

When Pasquala started to drape the new shawl over her head, Margarita snatched it away. "No! don't put it on yet. Not until the wedding. I have not worn mine."

Pasquala sighed. "How can I wait that long? But the

shawls are lovely. The blues are the blue of a happy sky. The yellow is as deep as the gold of our sunflowers. The brown is the warm brown in the robes Father Uria wears."

The wedding day finally came. Pasquala walked down the long aisle ahead of the happy bride. She tossed from her basket the tiny star flowers that meant happiness for Juan and Margarita.

But one shadow clouded even this day—the thought of the feathered warning. Pasquala was determined to let nothing cause her family to leave the mission. She felt that somehow she could do this. Was not her name Pasquala—one who helps other people?

7 | *The Piñons Are Ripe*

ONE November morning, about a month after the Harvest Fiesta, Pasquala's mother called her.

"Hurry, Pasquala," she urged. "Already the bells have stopped ringing. We must not be late."

Reluctantly, Pasquala crawled out from under the warm blankets. She would have liked to stay there a little longer, for the air was cool.

Near the door of the church, Jorge waited for her. "Luis came back," he told her eagerly. "Father Uria sent my brother up the high trail to see if the piñon nuts are ready. And they are. The trees are loaded."

Dismayed, Pasquala thought again of how close they would go to the village of the Tulares, when they went to gather the nuts in the piñon forest.

Jorge went on, his voice breaking into Pasquala's thoughts. "I hope Father Uria chooses me to go with you. It takes much strength to lift the heavy bags onto the burros." A gleam of mischief came into his dark eyes as he admitted, "Besides, it is easier than chopping weeds."

Pasquala stared down at the ground, avoiding his eyes. She did not want him to see how much Luis's report had upset her. "Picking nuts is hard work too," she reminded him solemnly. "And it's a long way—almost halfway to . . ." She stopped.

"Halfway to what?" Jorge asked.

"Why," she answered, hoping she had not given her anxiety away, "halfway to the high mountain peaks. It takes almost two days to get there."

"It *would* be a hard climb for women and girls," Jorge teased. A puzzled look crept into his eyes. He asked, "Don't you want to go?" When she said nothing, he went on. "Perhaps you'd rather work in the sewing room, or dip candles for old Pedro, our master candlemaker."

Without answering, Pasquala turned away and tried to catch up with her parents who had gone on ahead into the church. As she sat on the wooden bench, listening to the choir, she wondered if she would be chosen to gather the piñons. Since most of the women and children from the mission went, no doubt she and her mother would be asked to go.

The first thing that Father Uria spoke about in the schoolroom, later on that morning, was what Pasquala dreaded to hear. Jorge leaned forward. Pasquala knew he hoped to go as much as she hoped not to be included.

"I see that you have already heard the good news that Luis brought down from the piñon forest," Father Uria began. Some of the boys and girls giggled, anxious to be on their way. "You will leave at once. All the women except those with small children. I need the older boys to help me here. That is, all except one." He looked around the big, sunny room.

"Julio!"

A tall, broad-shouldered boy stood up.

"Since you are new to our mission and have never been to gather piñons, I thought perhaps you and your sister, Sara, might enjoy this holiday."

"Thank you, Father Uria," Julio answered.

Pasquala looked at Jorge at the other side of the schoolroom. His disappointment was plain to see.

Father Uria gave special work to the older boys and then he dismissed the children to get ready to go on the long trip into the mountains. They burst noisily out of the door.

All but Pasquala. She went quietly up the trail toward home, knowing it would be difficult to hide her worries from her mother.

Before long, the large group of women and girls and younger boys started up the trail that led to the piñon forest. Each carried a blanket tied to his shoulders. Some had empty reed baskets for gathering the nut harvest. Julio and Gregorio led the four burros up the winding path. On their backs the sturdy animals had several cooking pots, many bags to hold the nuts, and food for the journey.

Walking beside Pasquala, Sara said, "I'm glad Father Uria sent us on this holiday. I can hardly wait to taste the nuts. Where we lived we had no pine trees, or mountains."

Pasquala explained, "The piñon nuts are sweet and crisp. Everyone likes them."

Chatting with Teresa and Sara, Pasquala almost forgot her worries about being seen by a Tulare brave. But that night, as the group finally settled down, she had a hard time falling asleep. Wrapped in her blanket, she lay beside her mother watching the full moon come up over the high mountain peaks. She saw the twinkling stars and knew these same stars lit up both the mission and the village where her tribe lived.

At dawn, when everyone started to get up, Pasquala felt tired, having had little sleep during the night. But after eating a bowl full of hot chili beans in a thick meat sauce, she was ready for the day's climb.

Her mother helped Pasquala to tie on her blanket, and soon they started on their way again. The long line of women and children wound along the trail. Even the smallest boys and girls kept to the rapid pace set by the leaders.

That evening, tired out from the long, hard journey, and because she had not slept much the night before, Pasquala fell asleep at once. She threw an arm about her mother and did not awaken until dawn the next day.

Right after eating, the group started out again. At last, Pasquala's mother said, "It is not far now. We will soon see the large pine trees and enjoy the delicious piñon nuts."

Scarcely had the sun crept over the high ridge to the east when the harvesters arrived at the forest. Excited, the boys and girls raced about, delighted to be there.

"Luis was right," Pasquala said. She leaned down to pick up a handful of plump, brown nuts. "I have never seen so many before."

Sara cracked the thin shell of a piñon and bit into it.

"Um! They *are* good!" she exclaimed. "No wonder our Padre sends us on this long journey. These make the hard climb worth while."

After she had had quite a few, Sara went on, "I just can't stop eating them. They're delicious. But shouldn't we begin to fill our baskets?"

Pasquala grinned. Between bites, she said, "It's this way every year. We don't even start until after we've had all we can hold."

Teresa added, "No one prepares a meal for us on the first night at the forest. We're all too full of nuts to be hungry for beans."

As they talked, Pasquala's mother called to them. "We have work to do first, children."

Obediently, one by one the boys and girls crowded around her.

"By morning," she explained, "the wind gets strong and cold here. We must gather enough branches to make a windbreak. It will help to keep us warm while we sleep. Afterwards, you may go back and eat as many piñons as you wish."

Pasquala and the others brought the boughs as fast as Julio and some of the younger boys cut them. She kept a sharp lookout, ready to hide if a Tulare Indian came up the trail. But she saw only the eager harvesters.

When they had eaten all of the nuts they wanted, the

boys and girls began to fill their baskets. When these became full, they emptied them into one of the large cloth bags. By the time darkness came, everyone was glad to sleep behind the stout windbreak.

Once, during the blackness of the night, Pasquala heard the noise of snapping twigs. Fully awake, she propped herself up on one arm and stared into the dark. She listened, wondering if it was a deer prowling around for food. When the sound became softer and finally disappeared entirely, she lay down again and closed her eyes.

The next morning, after eating, everyone helped to gather the piñons. The hours went rapidly by. One after another bag became full to bursting with the delicious, sweet nuts. The women tied each bag securely at the top with strips of leather to keep the contents from spilling. Julio, with the help of two younger boys, stacked them to one side on the trail ready for loading onto the burros.

By sundown, the sky that had been clear and blue most of the day became full of dark gray clouds. These hung low, hiding the mountain peaks from sight.

Looking up at them, Sara's mother asked, "Are they snow clouds? But then, it does not snow here."

"Oh, but it does," Pasquala's mother assured her. "Usually not this early in the season. But this high up it often snows, although I have never been here when it did. Let us hope that it holds off until we start the long journey home."

About dawn the next morning, a fire was made to heat the food. This would give everyone the strength needed for the trip back.

With the help of the women, the boys loaded the patient little burros. Each heavy bag was finally strapped onto their backs. Leading the first one, Julio started down the path following Pasquala and her mother, who knew the way.

The children went along as fast as they could go. The older girls helped the tiny ones over the rough places in the trail. They all braced themselves against the strong wind that grew steadily colder and colder.

Shivering, Pasquala did not complain. She was only too glad to be going back to the mission.

All through that day and until late afternoon, the women and children followed the winding path down the mountainside. They stopped only long enough at noon to rest and eat.

That night they slept huddled together for warmth, sheltered somewhat by some huge rocks.

The next morning, they all grimly kept up the swift pace set by Pasquala's mother. Pasquala glanced up at the low clouds overhead. Their blackness worried her. She

hoped the snow would hold off a little longer, at least
until they were nearer the mission.

Completely exhausted, Pasquala fell asleep that night
as soon as she shut her eyes. Lying on the hard ground,
she felt chilled to the bone, although she had wrapped
herself in her warm blanket, close to her mother.

Cold, wet snow flakes melting on her face awakened
Pasquala long before dawn. She shook her mother and
whispered, "It's snowing. Already it covers the trail.
How will we find our way home?"

Gently, her mother soothed. "Do not be afraid. I

know the trail well. Besides, this is the first snow of the year. It probably won't amount to much. Farther down, the trail should be clear."

Most of the women and children were awakening. Sleepy-eyed, the boys and girls stood on the snow-covered trail, shivering in the icy wind that crept through their damp blankets.

Among themselves, the women agreed that they would not take the time to make a fire. They were anxious to start out as soon as possible because the snow would slow them up.

Without a word, Pasquala ate the cold beans her mother served her, even though they were tasteless. She knew that she needed the warmth and strength they would give her for the hard journey ahead.

Hours later, Pasquala asked her mother, "Have we taken the wrong path?"

Her mother cautioned, "Don't frighten the other children. I think we're on the right path. It's just that everything looks so different covered with snow."

After a while, as they took a sharp bend in the path, Pasquala's mother admitted, "I think now we are lost."

"*Lost!*"

They kept on. Pasquala hoped she would recognize something. But the narrow, twisting path was white with snow. Things did look different, as her mother said.

Suddenly, Pasquala's heart pounded with excitement. Not far away she saw a dead pine tree. She remembered it. Jorge had called it "the praying tree," because of the way two of its bent branches crossed in front of each other. Even covered with fluffy white flakes, Pasquala was sure it was the right tree.

Plucking her mother's blanket, she said, "I *know* where we are. I have seen that tree standing at the edge of the path." She pointed to it.

Pasquala's mother looked up at the old tree. "Are you sure, Pasquala?" she asked anxiously.

"Yes," Pasquala answered. "Once Jorge and Fernando and I went to hunt the roots Father Uria needed for the brown dyes. You remember? Well, that day, not far from that praying tree we found a cave. A big one. I told you about it. We could stay there until the storm is over."

Pasquala's mother said, "Yes, I remember now. How wonderful! A cave!"

The word spread rapidly along the line of harvesters that soon they would be safe and warm under the sheltering roof of a cave.

Slipping on the wet trail, Pasquala cautiously made her way around the praying tree. Just beyond it she pushed aside a tangle of brush. She stepped through the cave's entrance and smelled the damp, musty air inside. One by one, the eager children followed her, and they dropped down wearily on the hard, dry ground to rest.

But the burros, bulging with heavy bags, could not get through the small opening. Julio and the women unloaded the packs from the animals and led them inside. Then they dragged the bags of nuts in too, to keep them dry.

Julio said, "Find some twigs, and I'll start a fire."

"Then we can cook you a hot meal," his mother said, "and dry out our damp clothes."

The children did not take long to gather kindling. Julio bent over the pile with his flint and steel. At last he had a spark that flickered a moment, then burned with a strong, bright flame. They added heavier pieces of dry branches and before long the food was heated and ready for the hungry children.

Later, crowding around the warmth of the big fire, the boys and girls spread out their blankets and soon fell asleep. The women, too, gladly lay down to rest, grateful to be protected from the storm outside.

At dawn, when she awoke, Pasquala went to the cave's entrance. She looked down the trail and saw people hurrying toward her. She called out, "Here comes Father Uria, and I see Jorge and Fernando too."

Standing beside her, Julio said, "They must have worried about us when they saw all that snow on the peaks."

Joyfully, the children greeted their Padre. When he heard how Pasquala found the cave, he smiled down at her. Gently, he said, "I have named you well. You are, indeed, one who helps other people."

Wistfully, Pasquala hoped that she could always live up to her name.

Two months had passed since Jorge had buried the feathered warning, and Pasquala had not told her parents. Sometimes at night, when a strong gust of wind tossed the branches on the trees just outside the hut, she felt afraid. But then she would think again about Jorge's reassuring words, and her worries would go away.

On Christmas morning, Pasquala awoke long before dawn. She lay there looking up through the open window and watched the fading of the bright winter stars. How she loved living near the mission!

After the special holiday church service, Pasquala carried home the food for the first meal. Then she started toward the mission buildings. She had promised to help the boys get into their costumes for the Christmas play to be presented later on in the morning.

She met Jorge and Fernando on the trail.

Jorge said, "We've been waiting for you, Pasquala." He handed her a small wooden statue he had whittled. "Here is the figure of the Christ child Father Uria asked me to carve. Will you put it in the manger for me? Fernando and I have to cut more branches for the stage before we get into our costumes."

Pasquala ran a finger along the smoothness of the wood. She examined the tiny face with delight. "It is beautiful," she said. "It looks like a real baby—like your little brother."

"Yes, it does," Fernando broke in eagerly. "Jorge used him as his model."

After the boys went on their way, Pasquala hurried up the narrow path. At the last hut, where Fernando lived, she heard someone crying. Peeping into the room, she saw a little girl lying face down on her blankets. It was Carmen.

"Is something wrong?" Pasquala asked.

Carmen did not answer, and Pasquala reached down and turned her over. The child's cheeks were covered with tears, and her lips quivered. "Tell me what is wrong," Pasquala coaxed.

Seeing the carved figure in Pasquala's hand, Carmen's

eyes brightened. She sat up and reached for it. "Jorge wouldn't give me the doll he made, but you brought it to me. Thank you, Pasquala."

Pasquala did not like to disappoint the little girl, and she explained as gently as she could, "Jorge asked me to carry the statue to the stage, Carmen. The boys had to cut more branches and did not have time. How would you like to put the Christ child in the manger?"

Tears spilled down Carmen's cheeks again. "But I w-want t-to p-play with it. I want to put him to sleep under my blankets."

To comfort her, Pasquala said, "Maybe Father Uria will let you keep the statue after the Christmas play is over. I'll ask him."

This promise satisfied Carmen. Drying her eyes on her apron, she went with Pasquala. They walked through the patio and up the four steps to the platform that was the stage.

Pointing to the small reed basket in the left corner, Carmen said, "There, Pasquala. There's the manger."

"So it is," Pasquala agreed.

She picked up the cloth from inside the cradle and said, "Wrap him up, Carmen." Awkwardly, the child put the cover around it. Pasquala lifted Carmen up high enough so that the little girl could lay the figure inside.

Later, in the sewing room, Pasquala helped Jorge to

get into his costume. He looked different in the flowing
robes he wore for his part in the play. He had been
chosen to be the wisest of the Wise Men. He had the
only speaking part in the holiday pantomime.

"Unless you stand still, Jorge, I might prick you with
this pin," Pasquala said, annoyed with him.

Laura was having trouble with Luis, who was the
Satan of the play. Glancing over at the ugly mask that
hid his eyes, Pasquala shivered. It had the same ugly
lines she had seen on the face of old Nau-kloo, the evil
one.

Crossly, Laura said, "Unless you stop moving, Luis, I cannot fasten your mask. You don't want to lose it right in the middle of the pageant, do you?"

Luis reached over to yank playfully at her braids. "What a fussy old woman you are getting to be," he teased. "You'd think we were married."

Laura's face reddened. She stuck out her tongue at him. "If you're not ready in time, Father Uria will scold *me*."

When finally Jorge was ready, Pasquala helped Pablo, who was one of the eight angels. As she tied the last knot, she thought how very much like an angel he looked in his long white robes and the big, shiny wings.

During the past week, while Pasquala had helped to make the costumes, she had complained to her mother that the boys were always chosen to be in the Christmas play.

"I wish girls were allowed to take part too," she had said. "I would like to play the wisest of the Wise Men. I know every word. I listened to Jorge while he was learning them."

Glancing up now, Pasquala saw their Padre standing in the doorway. He motioned to her, and she hurried to his side. "I've been looking for you, Pasquala," he said, his face grave with concern. "I just spoke to Jorge. He said he gave you the figure he carved. Did you forget to put it in the manger? The play cannot begin until we find it."

Dismayed, Pasquala said, "But Father Uria, I did put it in the manger. It should be there on the stage. I don't understand what could have happened."

Father Uria shook his head. "It is gone!" Then he spoke to the boys and girls. "All those not in costumes will go and search for the little wooden figure Jorge carved. It *must* be found."

Pasquala did not go with the other children. She had an idea where to find it. Hurrying to the hut where Fernando and Carmen lived with their parents, she called out the child's name. No one answered. Then Pasquala looked inside and saw that the hut was empty.

Wondering what to do, Pasquala stood there a moment. She remembered having seen the little girl playing under a large pepper tree near the Santa Ynez River. There was a flat, smooth stone in the shade of that old tree, and Carmen often used it as a table for her acorn cups and saucers.

Hopefully, Pasquala ran along the winding path until she reached the river.

She called out, "Carmen, where are you?"

"Here!"

In a moment Pasquala stood beside her. On top of the stone lay the figure of the Christ child still wrapped in the piece of cloth from the manger.

Carmen put a finger to her lips and said, "Sh-sh-sh! He's sleeping."

Pasquala did not scold her. "Come with me, Carmen," she urged. "The Christmas play is going to begin soon. You don't want to miss it, do you? Father Uria wants us to bring this back right away." She picked up the statue and led Carmen by the hand along the path to the mission.

Later, after the play began, Pasquala sat quietly on the front bench, watching the colorful pantomime. She especially liked the music of the violins and flutes. The boys handled the instruments with great skill.

When the birth of Jesus was announced, Jorge said in a clear, serious voice, "A child is born—a savior!"

Finally Luis, as Satan, was forced off the stage by two angels, and the play ended. The evil lines of the ugly mask again reminded Pasquala of old Nau-kloo. But once more she put the thought of trouble from her mind.

9 | *The Arrow Race*

ONE winter afternoon, Pasquala sat with the other children in the schoolroom as Father Uria talked to them.

"It is a happy time of the year for us," he said. "Tomorrow is January the twenty-first, the feast day of Saint Agnes. As you know there are many preparations to be made. There will be many visitors to our mission. Some will come from as far away as the missions at Santa Barbara and San Gabriel to compete in our contests of skill."

Their Padre smiled at them as he went on. "I am too busy to hold the singing classes this afternoon. Instead, you may all have a holiday."

Delighted, the children murmured happily, "A holiday!"

When they had quieted down, Father Uria said, "I am sure the boys would like to practice for the hoop and javelins and for the stone toss. The girls will help Lucia in the kitchen to prepare the sweets that are served on the feast day of our patron saint."

The next day, after siesta, everyone went to the large field behind the mission walls where the contests would be held. Many visitors had camped close by, awaiting this moment. Each one hoped to win some of the prizes —fine saddles, beaded moccasins, colorful reed baskets and pottery bowls would go to those who won the various contests of skill.

Excited, Pasquala hurried toward the field, looking for Jorge. He was to ride Payuchi, the horse he had trained himself. She knew that he dreamed of winning the beautiful saddle that would go to the winner of the arrow race.

Glancing around at the crowds of people, Pasquala stopped suddenly, her heart beating faster and faster. A tall Indian walked toward her—the Tulare brave who had jumped out at her on the trail that day long before, calling her by her tribal name, Noktu! She could never forget him.

He did not even turn his head to look at Pasquala; but she had a feeling he had seen her. Had he come to compete in the games? Or had he come for something else!

Startled by the thunder of hoofs just behind her, Pasquala jumped out of the way. Jorge, on Payuchi, grinned down at her. The big horse reared, his front legs pawing the air. When he stood quietly, Pasquala reached up to pat him just above his quivering nose.

"His coat is as smooth as Father Uria's velvet ceremonial robes," she said.

"It should be smooth," Jorge answered. "I have brushed and brushed him. I wanted him to look his best."

"He does," Pasquala agreed. "Do you think he knows he's in the arrow race this afternoon?"

"Whether he knows it or not," Jorge said, "he will be. And we have practiced and practiced. Fernando and Payuchi and I have spent hours shooting the arrow through the hoop. I can pin the hoop down in practice. I only hope I can do it when the time comes."

Proudly Jorge pulled on the reins, turning his horse in a small circle. Pasquala could see how well her friend handled him.

"The saddle will look nice on Payuchi's back," she said.

Laughing, Jorge reminded her. "He has yet to win it. This is my first arrow race. Even though I have trained him, it takes much skill and courage to win. And it depends on Fernando too. On how well he throws the hoop."

"I've watched him practicing," she answered. "Fernando is the best of all."

"He's the best from Santa Ynez," Jorge agreed loyally, "but *is* he the best of all?" A gleam of mischief shone in his eyes.

Pasquala knew he was teasing her. She knew Jorge thought his friend Fernando could beat all contestants. She could see Jorge had no worries as far as the hoop throwing was concerned. He was thinking about his part—shooting an arrow through the hoop.

After he rode away, Pasquala walked toward the excited crowd. Sara waited for her.

Shyly, she said, "Pasquala, I have never seen an arrow race. Tell me about it."

"I think it is the most exciting race of all," Pasquala answered. "From horseback each rider aims his arrow so that it goes through a hoop thrown by another contestant. To win, the hoop has to be pinned to the ground by the arrow. If the arrow goes all the way through the hoop, the rider loses his chance to win."

"It sounds hard," Sara said, her eyes bright with expectation.

"It is," Pablo offered as he stood beside her. "It takes

skillful riding. The arrow must be shot at an angle. But my friends will win—Jorge and Fernando."

At last it was time for the arrow race. Pasquala thought her heart would burst with excitement. She was proud of the way Jorge guided Payuchi to the starting place. He handled his horse with great skill, the result of long hours of training.

Pasquala shaded her eyes against the bright sun with her hand. It was quite warm for a January day. She watched as one of the judges waved his arms to signal that the horses were ready. Another motioned to the crowd to back up out of the path of the contestants.

A third judge stayed near the line of hoop throwers to see that the horses did not slow their speed when they passed that point. Each rider must gallop all of the distance or be disqualified.

Fernando stood at the end of the long line of hoop throwers. Jorge, who was the youngest rider in the arrow race, came last of all.

One by one the visitors thundered by. Pasquala was glad that the young brave from the Tulare tribe could not compete in this particular game; her tribe was too poor to own horses.

At last, it was Jorge's turn. Twenty-two men had not been able to pin the hoop to the ground.

The starting judge signaled to Jorge. Fernando

waited, the hoop ready to throw, a determined look in his eyes.

Standing next to Pasquala, Sara whispered, "Oh, I hope Jorge wins."

"I hope so too," Pasquala answered. She heard Payuchi's thundering hoofs as he came nearer and nearer.

She saw Fernando get ready to throw the small wooden circle. It spun toward the middle of the path.

ZING!

Pasquala saw the feather-tipped arrow leave the bow. As Payuchi galloped past her, he stirred up clouds of dust. She could not see, but the cheers of the excited crowd told her that Jorge had won.

Pasquala and Sara and many others went to the table where the prizes were on display. They watched as Father Uria handed the saddle to Jorge. "Take it, my son," their Padre said proudly. "You have proved yourself to be a fine horseman. It pleases us all that you have brought this honor to Santa Ynez."

Jorge grinned. "Thank you, Father Uria. I would not have won if it had not been for Fernando. He threw the hoop at just the right time, and not too high or too low. That is a hard thing to do well."

Fernando smiled at this praise.

Later, Pasquala stood on the sidelines with Sara, watching the other games. But none was as exciting as the arrow race.

Both girls helped to serve the sweets to everyone. When they finished, Pasquala started for home, walking part of the way with Teresa and Sara.

Pasquala was surprised that she arrived home before her parents. She stepped into the dark hut and lit the candle on the table. Almost at once, she heard a slight movement behind her. Half turning, her lips formed the word "Mother." But a rough hand, covering her mouth, stopped any sound. Another hand pressed hard against her eyes.

Terrified, Pasquala twisted and turned. She was strong, but not strong enough to get away from the man. A cloth was forced between her teeth. The dirty gag made her feel sick.

Something soft was tied securely over her eyes, shutting out all light. She knew at once that the blindfold was the beautiful shawl Margarita had given her, the one she had worn so proudly the day Margarita and Juan were married.

Cruelly, her arms were yanked behind her back and leather thongs bound around her wrists several times. Her hands felt numb from the tight narrow strips that cut into her flesh.

Her captor lifted her, slinging her over his shoulder, head downward. The man left the hut and started up the trail that led to the Santa Ynez Mountains.

Before long, Pasquala's ears pounded from the blood rushing to her head. She wished the man would put her down and let her walk. But he kept on and on without seeming to tire. Up, up he went. She could hear him breathing hard as he climbed higher and higher.

At each step, Pasquala's head bumped against the man's hard, muscular back. The blindfold loosened, and she hoped her precious shawl would not fall off and get lost somewhere along the trail.

Once, when she almost slid off the man's shoulder, a rough hand yanked her back.

Pasquala wondered about her mother and father. Were they safe?

Then everything blacked out. When she regained consciousness, she was sitting on the ground, propped up against a tree, still gagged. But her blindfold was gone; her shawl had fallen off during the climb.

Behind her she heard the voices of several men. Her heart almost stopped beating when someone said to her captor, "So, you got Noktu! We have her mother here!"

By its high-pitched, nasal tone, she recognized the voice. Despair swept over her as she looked up and saw old Nau-kloo, the evil one!

FOUR years had passed since Pasquala had been kidnaped from Santa Ynez. They had been four sorrowing years spent among the Tulares, her people by birth. But she no longer felt that she belonged to the tribe, and she longed to be back at the mission.

Her mother had died shortly after their capture, and Pasquala missed her terribly.

Never once in all of these four years had Pasquala been left to herself for a single moment. When she went to gather berries in the foothills, or to find yucca roots for shampooing her hair, either her aunt or an old woman, Alaba, accompanied her. Her uncle told her this watchfulness protected her. He said many members of the tribe did not want her there and might harm her. Some resented having a Christian in their village.

Late at night, when she was certain no one could see her, Pasquala knelt down to say the words Father Uria had taught her. If she had been caught at her prayers, her uncle would have beaten her, as he had beaten her mother for refusing to give up the teachings of the mission Father.

Pasquala could only guess at what had happened to her father. Was he alive and well? Yet she knew, if he still lived, he would have come searching for her. Surely he had guessed that his brother and old Nau-kloo had had them both kidnaped from Santa Ynez.

Many times Pasquala thought about trying to escape, but she was guarded well. Once she had run off, but her uncle had sent swift runners who quickly caught her, and then he had beaten her. She had been too afraid to try again.

Of those in the village of the Tulares, only Alaba was kind. When Alaba went with her to gather berries or yucca roots, Pasquala braved the danger of a visit to the grave of her mother. The mound, overgrown with weeds, lay far from the village under an old oak tree. To Pasquala this small area of ground was as sacred as the burial place just outside the mission walls where the mission Indians had been laid to rest.

Whenever Pasquala dropped to her knees to pray,

Alaba always turned away, murmuring, as if to the empty air, "I see nothing. Only the eagle that flies overhead. Only the shadow the sun casts before me."

Pasquala was grateful for such a friend. She trusted Alaba to keep her secret.

No wooden cross marked the grave of her mother. Pasquala knew better. Her uncle would have trampled upon it had he seen it. Then he would keep her from coming ever again. Whenever she knew that she might have a chance to visit her mother's grave, Pasquala tucked a piece of leather thong in her blouse. With it she made a cross of twigs which she pushed into the dry, hard earth before she prayed. Afterwards, she took it apart so that no one would see it.

When the first streaks of sunlight showed through the smoke hole in the roof of the dwelling, Pasquala arose to start the fire to heat their food. From a leather thong about her waist hung a knife and a sewing bag. These she used in her duties during the day.

From a pile in one corner, Pasquala took dry grass and slivers of wood for kindling. Luckily, a few red coals still glowed in the deep pit, and she soon had a fire roaring, ready to cook the acorn soup.

As she worked, Pasquala heard the faint stirrings. Others in the village had awakened. Already, a few women were hurrying to the stream for water. Children stumbled sleepily into the sunshine.

When the morning meal was ready, Pasquala served her uncle and aunt. She forced herself to eat, knowing her uncle would scold her if she did not empty her bowl.

Later on Pasquala sat in front of the doorway enjoying the warmth of the winter sunshine. She smiled at Alaba who walked from her own tent to talk to them.

The women rested from their chores, but Pasquala kept busy. She mended a pair of calfskin leggings that her uncle had torn on his last deer hunt.

Always Pasquala did her work willingly and well. Often her aunt said, "They taught you well at the mission. You will be a good wife to a brave when the time comes."

Four years had changed Pasquala. She had grown taller and thinner. Her eyes no longer shone with happiness, but reflected her longing to return to Santa Ynez. Only at the mission could she be really happy and content.

Many times Pasquala thought about the busy, joyful days she had spent at her beloved mission. How she wished she could see another Christmas play, another Harvest Fiesta. How she wished that she could visit Margarita and Juan in their home.

Pasquala's uncle strode up to her. "Noktu," he ordered crossly, "you and Alaba find some herbs for the medicines. Old Nau-kloo needs them."

Obediently, Pasquala and Alaba went. Pasquala carried both baskets. Carefully, she matched her youthful steps to the slow, steady plodding of the old woman. With the same thought, they turned toward the familiar oak tree.

When they reached the grave, Alaba said, "If you hurry, we can stop. We can make up the lost time easily enough."

Pasquala kissed the wrinkled hand gratefully. "Thank

you, Alaba. I hoped you would let me come here first."

Alaba said, "It is a long time since we came. It may be a long time until we come again."

"I'll hurry!" Pasquala promised. "I would not have you get into any trouble because of me."

Alaba looked steadily into Pasquala's eyes. "You have been a thoughtful daughter to me—a daughter the Great Spirit never sent. You have always been kind, as your mother was kind. You have listened when this old woman spoke. Although I do not believe your way, I see that it comforts you. I can do so little in return for your sweetness to me."

Quickly, Pasquala made a cross of twigs, setting it in the earth. Her eyes closed out the wide stretches of the valley and the distant mountains. She imagined herself once more in the mission chapel.

She prayed for the dead as she remembered Father Uria praying, trying to use some of the words he had spoken.

Behind her, facing the foothills, Alaba murmured clearly, "I see nothing. Only the eagle that flies overhead. Only the shadow the sun casts before me."

Suddenly, Alaba grabbed Pasquala's arm, pulling her to her feet. She pointed to the figure of a man coming quickly from the direction of the village.

"Come, child," Alaba urged. "My aged eyes are as sharp as a spotted fawn's. Here comes old Nau-kloo, the troublemaker."

11 | *The Warpath*

For a moment Pasquala stood still, too frightened to move.

Again Alaba urged, "Hurry, child."

In her breathless haste to follow the old woman, Pasquala tripped over her skirt, falling on the stony ground. Scarcely realizing that she had skinned an elbow and knee, she scrambled to her feet. Grabbing the baskets, she hurried after Alaba.

After putting a safe distance between them and the aged oak tree, Pasquala stopped to look back. Old Naukloo had reached the grave, pausing for a moment. Then, as she watched him anxiously, he turned and headed back to the village.

Had the medicine man been sent to spy on them?

To make up for the lost time, Pasquala picked herbs as fast as she could. Toward sunset, she and Alaba had filled both of the baskets full to their brims. They started back. When Pasquala reached her uncle's dwelling, her aunt had already prepared the evening meal.

As she ate, Pasquala stared out the open doorway, watching as many men hurried toward the council tent. She asked her aunt, "Are there religious ceremonies tonight?"

Instead of answering her question, Pasquala's aunt turned away, stooping down to throw a few sticks into the fire pit. Pasquala wondered if the braves could be preparing for the warpath. But she had not heard talk of war. She felt sure Alaba would have told her. The old woman chatted constantly about the village news.

Breaking into her thoughts, Pasquala's aunt finally said, "Your uncle will be late for the evening meal. He holds a powwow."

A powwow usually meant war! Pasquala's heart beat faster. War was evil. Men should not kill. If only her tribe could be made to see how wonderful it was to live the peaceful life of mission Indians.

Later, when her uncle came into the dwelling, Pasquala served him the food she had kept warm over a low fire. He ate slowly, and, as he ate, she stood to one side ready should he need anything.

When he finished, he looked over to where she waited. "Noktu," he said, his voice harsh and loud.

Alarmed, Pasquala stared at him, wondering why he was angry with her.

"Nau-kloo stopped at your mother's grave today. He found something that should not have been there."

Pasquala searched her mind frantically. Then she gasped in despair, remembering. She had forgotten the little cross.

Terrified, Pasquala watched her uncle as he held out the twigs still tied together with the piece of thong.

"Many times," he went on, "I have told you to forget the teachings of that Padre. Because you were young I did not have you killed as I should have done. I thought when you came back to our village you would forget the foolish words spoken by your Father Uria. I kept hoping you would again follow the beliefs of our tribe. But you have not."

As if in a stupor, Pasquala heard her uncle's anger against her. "You were born to this tribe. You are a member of this tribe. I have been patient with you. But you are old enough now to know that the teachings of that mission Christ are as the dust under your feet."

Pasquala pressed her lips together, trying to hold back the words she wanted to say. Finally, she blurted out, "You're wrong. Wrong! The life at the mission was happy. I will *never* forget what Father Uria taught me, not if you beat me."

As soon as she had spoken, Pasquala realized she had made a dreadful mistake letting her uncle know how she felt. He glared at her, his eyes blazing with hatred.

Almost shouting, her uncle went on, "Your father, my brother, accepted the mission life against my wishes. Against me, his chief. Five times I sent messengers to tell your father to return to his own tribe, or there would be trouble." A crafty, evil look came over his face when he added, "Well, there was trouble. And there will be more trouble."

Pasquala heard his next words without realizing their awful truth immediately. "As chief of the Tulares I made an example of my own brother."

And then Pasquala knew that her father was dead. She sank weakly to the ground and covered her face with her arms.

Now she was alone. All alone. Hope of some day having her father come for her was gone forever.

"I am at the end of my patience, Noktu," her uncle

said. "I expected you to forget the mission. Perhaps you will forget if . . ."

In spite of herself Pasquala looked up at him and asked, "If *what?*"

"If I help! Suppose there was no mission. No Father Uria. Would you forget then?"

He glared down into her frightened eyes. There was no mistake now about what he planned to do.

Grabbing him around his knees, she begged, "Oh, no! No! Don't hurt my Padre. Don't burn the mission."

"I see you understand me," he replied. "That is a much better way to stop this nonsense; much better than beating it out of you. I have old Nau-kloo to thank for suggesting the plan we will follow."

He stared at the twig cross a moment, then with a quick toss it landed in the embers of the fire.

"There," he cried, his anger filling the tent. "That is what should happen to all symbols of a faith that interferes with the ways of our tribe."

Without looking back, he strode through the doorway. Pasquala sank to the ground again. With a growing horror she watched the little cross flame up for a short instant, then die down. What should she do? What *could* she do?

The twig cross finally broke up among the ashes and

became a part of them. Only the strip of leather remained in the red coals. It was as if her beloved mission itself already lay in ruins. That must not happen. Father Uria must not be harmed. Jorge, Fernando and many more of her good friends might die in the battle.

Speaking to Pasquala, her aunt urged, "Come, child. It is time to sleep. Nothing you can do will stop your uncle, now that the war rites have begun."

Obediently, Pasquala lay down on her bed mat. She closed her eyes, but she remained wide awake, thinking. She had to save Father Uria, and the mission, and all of the good people who lived at Santa Ynez. She had to. There must be a way to help them.

She prayed, and, as she prayed, all doubt suddenly left her. She knew what she had to do. This very night, with the full moon to light her way, she would start the long journey across the high mountains and tell the Padre of the coming attack. Perhaps the few soldiers at the mission would be able to hold out against the warriors if they were warned in time.

Lying there, Pasquala felt afraid, remembering how her uncle had beaten her the first time she tried to escape. What if they caught her again and brought her back? But she was four years older now and much stronger, and she could go faster.

Pasquala knew that the Tulares never went on the warpath until they had taken the night-long sweat baths. That was where her uncle was now, and he would not be back again that night. Early in the morning, before dawn, the braves would leave the steam tents and start the exhausting war dance that lasted from sunrise to sunset. Only then would they start out, eager for battle.

These lengthy preparations would give Pasquala nearly a day's head start. Once the rites started, they would not miss her. When the ceremonies ended, the Tulares might guess where she had gone and what she planned to do; but the swift warriors, realizing she did not know the trail, would confidently expect to catch up with her.

Not until the moon shone down through the smoke hole in the roof did Pasquala's aunt sleep soundly. At last, she breathed deeply and steadily. The time had come to leave.

Quietly, Pasquala slipped her feet into her moccasins. From a basket near the doorway, she filled her sewing bag full of meal cakes and dried deer meat. Much food would be needed for the long journey ahead.

Moving as silently as a cloud across the sky, Pasquala crept through the door flap. She made her way past one tent after another. Finally, she reached the edge of the village. A dog raised his head to sniff at her, but he did not bark.

A long stretch of flat plains lay between her and the mountain trail. Before someone could see her crossing them, Pasquala dashed for the dark foothills in the distance.

PASQUALA raced through the bright moonlight toward the foothills. She kept on and on, not daring to stop while she was still on the flat plains, for there someone might see her.

Even when she was hidden from sight on the twisting mountain trail, Pasquala did not slow up. As she ran, she listened, expecting to hear the sound of footsteps behind her. Before long Pasquala was gasping for breath. But she pushed on. The pain in her side was hard to bear, but she did not stop to rest.

Finally, as the moon faded in the dawn light, Pasquala dropped exhausted on the ground, cradling her head in her arms. She waited only long enough for her breath to get back to normal, then she started out once more.

As she climbed, she ate an acorn cake and some of the dried deer meat to give her strength.

All through the day, Pasquala went on, not daring to stop again. Only when darkness came and a thick gray mist hid the trail did she sit down wearily. Leaning against a tree at the edge of the winding path, she slept until dawn.

Again, Pasquala hurried on her way, climbing up, up, coming nearer and nearer to the top of the high mountains. The grave need to bring the warning in time made her fairly fly along the trail. She was glad the braves must climb the mountains on foot too. The tribe was so poor that not even her uncle, their chief, owned a horse. Perhaps this would give her a chance to reach the mission before they did.

Suddenly Pasquala stopped, listening. The sound of sliding stones on the path behind her made her heart pound in her chest. Terrified, she stood still. As the sound came nearer, she hid behind a large piñon tree, waiting to see what was making the noise. It did not seem likely that a brave would betray his presence in that way. He would come silently.

A large buck walked gracefully toward Pasquala. When he sensed her nearness, he wheeled and leaped back into the underbrush and disappeared.

Once more Pasquala started toward the peaks high above her. Through the morning and afternoon, she kept on. She did not even stop at night until heavy clouds hid the moon, and the trail became too dark to follow.

Before she slept, Pasquala prayed that she would reach the good Padre in time. If she could warn him, he might be able to save the mission and the many people who lived near it.

The next morning, Pasquala arrived at a place where two paths came together. Both had been worn smooth by the moccasins of Indians and many animals who followed it. She did not know which way to go. If she chose the wrong one, she would arrive, not at her beloved Santa Ynez, but at the shores of the Sunset Ocean.

Pasquala knelt down. She prayed to be guided along the right path. When she opened her eyes, she looked down at the ground just in front of her. Something white shone through the dry leaves. With eager, excited fingers Pasquala brushed aside the earth until she had uncovered three large pebbles, set in a straight line.

Her tired mind wearily forced itself back, year by year, until she was a little girl again, a girl of five. More and more clearly she remembered about the pebbles. They marked the trail to the Sunset Ocean.

Joyfully, Pasquala spoke aloud. "Now I know which way to go. The mission will be in the other direction."

As she climbed higher and higher, Pasquala shivered in the damp fog that clung to the treetops. She wished that she had brought a blanket with her. But a blanket would have been too heavy to carry. More than warmth she needed speed if she hoped to get to the mission in time.

Toward noon, Pasquala reached the crest of the mountains. From now on the trail would be mostly downward. She would be able to go much faster now.

That night, too tired to go further without rest, Pasquala leaned up against a tree and shut her eyes. But she slept fitfully. She felt hot one moment and cold the next, exactly as she had with the fever long ago. She dreamed she was back at the mission and that their Padre was curing her again.

She awoke more rested and started out once more. As she went down the trail, she ate the rest of the food. Now she would have to depend on winter apples she would find along the way for the strength she would need for the journey.

At the end of that day, Pasquala came to the edge of a small bubbling spring. She wondered if it was one of the many streams that flowed into the Santa Ynez River. If so, she was truly on the right trail to the mission.

Too tired to take another step, Pasquala lay down on the ground to rest a while. Then she prayed for the strength to get her to the mission. Finally, she fell into a deep sleep.

Pasquala dreamed of hearing the clear, sweet bells calling her to church. She even heard the music of the flutes and violins and the beautiful voices of the boys' choir.

Sleepily, she wondered what Jorge had done when her uncle had her kidnaped from the mission. She remembered how kind Margarita had been to weave a fine shawl for her—the one Pasquala had lost on the trail that terrifying day four years before. Perhaps Margarita and Juan had children of their own by now.

When Pasquala opened her eyes the next morning, she heard mission bells. Was she still dreaming? No! She did not dream this. Her ears told her this was true. The air was filled with the sweet music of the faraway bells, the bells of Santa Ynez. She had heard them too many times to be mistaken.

As she hurried down the trail, Pasquala was startled by the sound of sliding stones. Would someone catch her? Not waiting to find out, she went faster and faster and faster. When she came to the path that led down the steep canyon wall, she was greatly relieved. She took this short cut to the valley below, knowing it would save many precious moments.

When a low branch tore her skirt near the bottom edge, tripping her, she stopped only long enough to rip the piece off. As she slid down the rocks and cliffs, she glanced back once to see if the warriors had caught up with her; but she saw no one on the trail above.

Reaching the floor of the valley, Pasquala stood looking straight ahead at the river shining in the early-morning sunlight. She recognized the place where Jorge and Fernando went spear fishing. Not far below it was the small cove where she had fallen into the Santa Ynez.

Hurrying toward the swift river, Pasquala knew that soon she should see the beloved red-tiled roofs gleaming brightly, and she prayed for the strength needed to reach them.

13 | *The Message for Father Uria*

PASQUALA followed the high banks of the Santa Ynez. In a short while she turned away from the river and started to cross the wheat fields.

Then she saw a tall young man standing nearby, a hoe in his hands. He stared in her direction, then flung the tool from him. He strode toward her, a questioning look on his face.

It was Jorge. Her good friend, Jorge, no longer a boy but a man. Stumbling in her eagerness, Pasquala called out to him. "It is I, Jorge—I, Pasquala."

As she swayed from weariness, he caught her up in his strong arms. "I can't believe it is you, Pasquala. I had prayed."

At the end of her strength, Pasquala gasped, "Take me to Father Uria. Quickly!"

"Yes, Pasquala!" He cradled her in his arms and strode toward the mission buildings. "Have you come from your tribal village?"

"Yes," Pasquala answered softly. "I bring an urgent message for Father Uria."

"I don't see how you came that far," Jorge said, great respect in his voice.

"Tell me about my father, Jorge," Pasquala said.

A grim look crossed the young man's face. His voice held a deep sadness as he answered, "It is not good news, Pasquala. We found him. After he died, I made a fine wooden cross for his grave."

Walking through the main gate, Jorge continued, "Fernando and I found your shawl on the trail, and I kept it for you, hoping you'd come back some day. I wanted to go all of the way to your village to get you back, but the Padre said no. He reminded me to 'love my neighbor,' not harm him. Our Padre wanted no blood shed."

Going past the church, Jorge found Father Uria in his private garden, tending his beloved flowers.

"Here's Pasquala, Father," Jorge announced. "Pasquala has come back to Santa Ynez."

"God be praised!" Father Uria said, looking down into her tired face. "She must be given a chance to rest.

Come! Carry her to the cell at the end of the north corridor."

Led by their Padre, Jorge walked into the small room and laid Pasquala on the narrow cot. But she sat up. "I came to . . ."

"Rest, child," Father Uria urged. "Rest first. You have come far. We'll hear about your experiences when you feel a little stronger."

"But Father," she persisted. "I must not sleep until I speak. I came to warn you. My uncle plans to come here. To burn the mission. Kill you!" She collapsed weakly against the mattress.

"Rest now, Pasquala," Father Uria said. Turning to Jorge, he ordered, "Go and tell the sergeant in charge about this. Have him send someone to the Mission Santa Barbara for more soldiers. Hurry!"

After it was all over, Pasquala found out that she had slept for a day and a half. When she awakened,

she heard a knock on the door. Jorge entered arm he carried her shawl.

"I brought this, Pasquala," he began. "I thought you might like to have it again."

"Oh, thank you, Jorge," she said, smiling at him.

A moment later, Father Uria came into the room. He said, "You are truly our savior, Pasquala. Had you failed to warn us in time, we would have lost many of our people. After just one volley from the guns of our soldiers, the warriors turned away and crept back up the mountains without shooting one poisoned arrow; without setting fire to one of our buildings. Had it not been for your bravery, Santa Ynez might have been entirely destroyed."

Father Uria went on soberly, "I shall write all this in the mission records, my child. All those who come after will know about the Indian girl who made the incredible journey alone over the high mountains to save our mission."

When the Padre left, Jorge asked, "Is there something I can do for you, Pasquala?"

"Yes," she answered. "I still feel weak. Will you help me to the chapel? I have not seen Saint Agnes for four long years."